SIDEWINDER: A NOVELLA

Cover design by Darya @antiquedeuce

Name: Haddad, Marcella, author.

Title: Sidewinder / Marcella Haddad

Description: First Edition / St. Peters, MO: Gateway Literary Press [2023]

First Edition Paperback July, 2023

Published by Gateway Literary Press

gatewayliterarypress.wordpress.com

SIDEWINDER: A NOVELLA

MARCELLA HADDAD

Gateway Literary Press

for Caleb

I love you always

SIDEWINDER

The first city to get eaten was San Brado. Vago and I were on watch when the survivors approached our fort on a dustier-than-usual afternoon, coalescing out of the desert like black birds. The first was tall and pale and wore her hat low, a scarf covering the bottom half of her face. The second was wide and brown. Her eyes darted around as if she could spot some invisible threat in the sand. Both of them had regulation rifles slung over their shoulders, though I didn't see a speck of ammunition between them.

They stopped in front of the gate. The tall one tilted her hat up to take in the full height of our fort walls. San Orgafi cuts a pretty dramatic sight in the middle of the long desert. Our walls are twelve-feet tall, sharpened spikes of wood tied together tighter than braids, pure black from ash.

"Go ahead and show us your travel papers," Vago said, chewing his leaf and not even making a threatening movement towards his pistol.

The women didn't answer at first. Maybe they were outlaws. A while back, when I first took on watch, I used to accept bribes. San Orgafi is a waystation, one of the few stops on the long road west. Most people without their papers only wanted some rest and food before getting on their way. I would even direct them to Tila Igala's little stand where she would fix them up fried dumplings and plantains in the dark, her fire hidden between the chapel and the wall, out of sight of the official visitors and citizens.

I used to wonder what Mama would say if she were still here. If she'd tell me to be like Tifero, insisting on double-checking documents, or to be understanding towards those who traveled far. I didn't think I was causing much trouble letting strangers in. You can call it my weak woman's heart but I call it my man's greed. I don't feel like either one of those most times, just a creature making some sort of justice and also some nice cash. Then things got a little murdery around here. Now I don't question or bend. No in or out without the right paperwork.

"If not, there's still time to turn back before sunset, maybe reach San Brado if you move quick," I said to the travelers.

"San Brado's gone," the shorter woman said. Still, neither of them made any move towards producing papers, so I rested my hand on my own pistol.

"Surely it'll reappear again once you cross that horizon." Vago jutted his sharp chin towards the road behind them, where the endless red sand met the pale sky.

"Surely it'll be a chasm in the shape of a coyote bite," the same woman said. "An emptiness where it all used to be."

It took both of us a moment to register her words. My first instinct was to worry about Tifero, who left to re-supply in San Brado a week ago. Then Vago threw his head back and laughed, and I realized the strangeness of what they had said. I loosened my grip on my pistol.

"We don't have room for mad folk here," I said in what I hoped was a gentle tone. "Whatever misfortune has befallen you, we can't help."

"We are here to help *you*." Now the white woman spoke, pulling down her scarf. The wind tugged out wisps of her blonde hair. "We escaped and now we're warning the other forts. The great creatures are stirring. There should still be time for you to evacuate."

"From what, a giant coyote? Big enough to bite a city?" Vago laughed again, imitating the creature's *yip* and then snapping at the air in front of him. He isn't usually so cruel but sometimes the long days of our unending watch get to him.

"You'll have a hard journey if you mean to reach the next eastern fort," I said, gesturing at their apparel. "You don't have any bullets left, no sign of provisions, and hardly dressed for the desert with that much black. What do you plan to do against the outlaws on the road? Against the venomous creatures? Against the sun?" I wanted them to reassure me, to reveal what secret supplies or help they had. My weak heart again.

The shorter one answered. "We have greater things to fear now."

Vago only gave them an unworried smirk.

The taller woman raised her scarf again after sending us a glare, and put her hand on her companion's arm, leading her away. As protocol dictates Vago and I followed them along the black walls as they walked around San Orgafi to the other side, continuing east down the road.

I watched as they became distant and small, flecks of

pepper absorbed in the doughy desert. Damn. I really did get too hungry the longer I was on watch.

"Seja." Vago nudged my shoulder, and I lost sight of them completely. I turned to see my friend fixing his hair, straight and black down past his chin, and often pulled back from his face. Though there were always those two insistent strands in the front that would never stay put behind his ears. "Been awhile since you looked like that."

"Like what?" I rubbed dust out of my eyes, glancing up at the arc of the sun to see how much longer our watch was.

"Your waiting-face," Vago said, and offered me his flask.

Most people don't mention Mama, don't mention her leaving, don't mention what I was like after she left. But Vago saw all of it. He told me once that during the months after, he wondered how I could sit so still on watch, eyes eating up the horizon like I was starving.

"Don't want to get distracted while we're on duty." I pushed aside his flask, even though in the past I'd certainly had my share of leaf and spirits to add texture to the monotony of watch. "And I'm not waiting for anything now."

*

I've never gotten much help from holy folk but my Mama went to them for a reason. I wasn't too keen on seeing the Preacher again after our last conversation years ago, but there's nothing like madwomen spouting images of world-eating creatures to make you a bit concerned about your Heavenly Soul.

The noses of proper citizens turned up at my dust-red coat

and my hair, chopped into tufts around my ears that stuck out under my hat. I had enough grace to at least remove that. I slid into a pew and ignored the trail of dirt left behind by my boots.

Our Preacher is pious enough to have cheated death, or at least looks like it, with the amount of wrinkles she's collected. Her eyes always seemed empty to me. Either a woman who has seen too much suffering or too little. Her voice echoed high and low in the chapel, wrapping her words around the white-oak rafters and twining through the dusty feathers on ladies' hats. She painted visions of the Heavens for us, summoning wide green leaves dripping with dew and fanged animals soft and gentle and at our command.

"What wonders await us in the next life," she said. "If only we avoid temptation in this one. If we follow the Holy Word and not our own desires. If we value the path of the Heavens and not the path that others put upon us."

I was surprised with how much I liked her sermon, or maybe what I liked was the time to daydream. The uninterrupted desert and black fort walls don't usually provide a soul with much inspiration. I couldn't read but I opened the Holy Book to one of the grand illustrations. I liked the page with the River of the Next Life. The river came down from the clouds and into a city, a real city with towers and not a fort, and there were bodies in the river. They looked dead.

"They like to make those drawings so macabre, don't they?" said a deep whisper, and I was so startled that I threw the book up in the air and then the ground pulled it right back down with a blasphemous clatter.

In the silence when the Preacher and everyone else who

was penitent turned to stare at me, I looked over at the rightful culprit.

He had black hair and barely tamed brows, skin shining brown-gold as if embers were just beneath the surface, the typical sheen of sweat cast over every visitor to San Orgafi. He had nice clothes, too nice for a fort in the middle of nowhere — a violet vest over a white shirt with the sleeves rolled up. Now at least that was properly dirty.

The worst thing about him was his barely restrained grin, knowing that everyone was looking at me and not him. I hate that expression, when folks get away with something they know they shouldn't have.

My hand strayed to my hip, though of course I'd left my pistol at the front of the church. It was the only weapon in the bucket set aside for them. Most folk who aren't watchers or outlaws don't need weapons inside the fort, but I sure wished I had mine now. Not to use it, but to reassure him that I knew how.

The stranger raised one eyebrow, glancing down at my trigger-hand and back up at my face. He didn't bend his perfect posture as he peered back down at his own Holy Book with a smile. The perfect pious citizen. I could tell by the flit of his heavy lashes that he was actually reading, like a show-off.

The Preacher cleared her throat and tugged the other eyes back to her as she continued reading a poem from the Holy Word. I continued staring at the stranger as if he were a stray dog outside the gate that I could scare off. Maybe he could feel my eyes trained on him like a rifle — he kept his little smile on the side of his mouth the whole time.

When the sermon finished and the others filed into the aisle like a river to speak with the Preacher, I waited for the stranger to look up and see my glare. Instead, he was already striding towards the end of the pew, replacing his black hat and ducking between two ladies in pastel-green skirts. He nodded politely as he moved past and they turned towards him like flowers facing the sun. I moved to follow when a heavy hand landed on my shoulder.

"Seja." The Preacher smiled and revealed cloud-white teeth. "I'm happy to see you."

I shifted in my boots, glancing towards the door where the stranger had disappeared, and back at the murmuring crowd gathered at the front of the church.

"I think there's a lot of folks waiting to talk to you," I said.

"And I need to talk to *you*." The Preacher led me down the black pews to her prayer room. From the outside of the chapel it looked like a small turret, out of place, the only whimsical architecture in all of San Orgafi. While I was admiring the curving walls the Preacher took one of my hands in both of hers. "You never returned to me."

I liked to think it was impressive that I'd been able to avoid her in a town this small for so many years, but instead of bragging I swallowed that thought and just lowered my head.

The Preacher leaned in. "Have you had visions?"

"No," I said quickly. "Not at all." I hesitated to trust the Preacher, but I had come here for a reason. "But there were two travelers this morning."

"And they had a warning." The Preacher pulled me further into the shadows, and the curve of the wall dulled the chatter of the congregation. "Tell me."

"I think they were going mad, Preacher," I said at first.

She nodded slowly. I shivered. This room must be the coldest place in San Orgafi. I hated the whole chapel, but it was still part of my little city. I didn't want any of it to get eaten. I told her what the travelers had said about San Brado and the coyote.

"The size of a city," she mused, looking back out at the chapel.

"I didn't mean to waste your time with nonsense," I said, feeling the same anxious desire to escape as I had the last time I'd set foot in this place.

"There was a time when all the great creatures who began the world fell asleep." The Preacher seemed to be looking beyond the chapel now, beyond San Orgafi, beyond our desert. "Of course, mortal deeds did not give them easy dreams. First they were restless. Now they are awake." She brought her gaze back to mine, ignoring the confused frown twisting my lips. "Thank you for telling me, dear Seja. Now is the time to have faith."

"Faith in false tales?" I said, echoing Tila Igala.

"Faith in yourself." The Preacher folded her hands into mine. "I know the gift hasn't manifested in you yet, but...if there was ever a time..." Her grip tightened. "Now you must continue your studies. This is beyond you and your little world, Seja. I let you waste your time on the watch for too long."

I pulled my hand out of hers. I felt unbalanced in the shadows, without the weight of my pistol, under the feverish gaze of the woman who had taken my Mama away from me.

"I'm doing more good on the watch than I would in

here, Preacher," I said. "Seems I have a lot of mad folk and fearmongering to protect my 'little world' from."

I stalked out of that shadowy tower, down the aisle of pews, afraid she would follow me. Then I got angry at the thought. What could that little old woman do to me? No more than she already had.

I pulled my pistol out of the weapon bucket, letting it clang against the sides. Offended titters erupted behind me but I don't think folks have a right to complain about the demeanor of someone who's just trying to keep them safe.

Outside the chapel, under the sun, I felt better. Here were people more similar to me than the worshippers. Dirty, dusty, carrying weapons and wariness. Lots of travelers but you could always spot the locals — they owned the shadows, taking up the only cool spots out of the heat. The wooden storefronts always seemed to lean forward or to the sides a few more inches each year, and most had a balcony on the second story. That's where you could spot the rich folk sweating in all their beautiful silk.

My next watch didn't start till after sunset but I strode towards the wall anyway. That was the best place to avoid anything and anyone, in between the black wood and the backs of buildings. But the Heavens must have been upset at my disruptions in the chapel so they decided to disturb my own peace.

Someone was following me.

I was more annoyed than afraid. I could sense them on the back of my neck, but mostly I could tell by the whispers and glances of the folks on either side of me. A lady looking up from under her hat, a gunslinger whispering to his companion on a balcony. I knew who they were looking at. He didn't deserve the dignity of a quiet confrontation.

I turned around in the middle of the street, pushing my coat aside to reveal my pistol at my hip. I didn't want to make the citizens uncomfortable by pulling it out but I sure was itching for a reason to.

The stranger from the chapel slowed down as he approached, raising his hands by his head. His smile was a little too satisfied for it to look like a real surrender.

"An impressive weapon," he said.

"It's for untrustworthy folk like you." He'd found the only angle of flattery that could possibly weaken me. I did love my pistol, but I wasn't going to let myself get tempted into a conversation about its efficient reloading mechanism.

The insult bothered him less than a fly. "Why did the Preacher want you to return to her?"

Now that, I was not expecting. "Why didn't you ever learn not to eavesdrop?"

His grin was wide. "It's part of my occupation, I'm afraid."

I squinted at him. What was he, some kind of spy? He was dressed far too nice to be a regular runaway or outlaw — they knew better than to showcase any wealth. He must work for some powerful folk. "Who let you in?"

"You want to know so that you can go interrogate your colleagues?" He lowered his hands now, and I considered pulling out my pistol just to remind him to stay on guard. "I'm happy to provide my papers again, if you insist on doing your job even off-duty. I admire your commitment to your town." He still had that satisfied, entitled expression.

"What kind of business do you have in San Orgafi?" I said,

since it seemed he was here officially. "And more importantly, when is it finished?"

"My business is with a beautiful girl," he said. His face was sharp, dark eyes under angular brows in a shape I'd never seen before. They were brown, like some kind of ancient tree that could never grow out here in the heat. Gun to my head I would admit he was handsome. Luckily he didn't seem to have one.

"Well, I'm not a girl," I said. "Not a man either."

"A beautiful gunslinger, then." His gaze turned serious. "You're Seja Bela Arantija."

I winced. "The middle name was unnecessary."

"I want you to understand that I am a thorough man," he confessed. "I have been looking for you."

That anyone outside of this little place, outside of this desert, could know anyone in San Orgafi, let alone me, was the strangest thing to occur in all my years. Even stranger than great city-creatures stirring.

He said his next words delicately. "Your mother is Maron Abej Arantija."

My hand fell. I let my coat flutter shut over my pistol. "Mama sent you?"

The stranger stepped closer, looking pained. He raised his hand as if to embrace me in the same empathetic habit that Tila Igala had with any child. "You have no idea how tempting it is to let you believe that."

Mama.

"Seja!"

I was startled at the sound of my name because the stranger's lips hadn't moved, still pressed together with concern, and for a second I thought his voice was somehow in my head. Then I saw Vago stride down the steps of the saloon. He let his boots land heavy on the creaking wood.

"Who's this?" he said, cocking his head in what most around here know is a dangerous look. Vago's soft once you know him, but before that he's got a mean face.

I opened my mouth to reply, but what was I going to say? This is a man who knows Mama but she didn't send him, she doesn't care about me, so he's not really that important?

"Kamyar Eirvad," the stranger said, holding out his hand to Vago. A spiral of black ink on his wrist snuck out from under his sleeve.

Kamyar Eirvad. I silently tasted the unfamiliar vowels. When I looked up the owner of the name was watching my lips, that little smile back again. Damn.

Vago grasped his hand, shook it hard, leaving a dark smudge of dirt on the stranger's sleeve.

"Heading west?" Vago guessed. It was a fair assumption. It was the direction those with money traveled in. East was for those who had given up, were heading back.

Like the strangers from San Brado.

I looked back at the pointed teeth of the wall as it bit into the setting sun. What had they really seen?

"Staying in San Orgafi for now," Kamyar Eirvad said smoothly, as if that wasn't something that would make us automatically suspicious of him. "My research brings me here."

"Ah, a scientist?" Vago said, and I could tell he was getting tired of the conversation, edging into the slightly cruel teasing that kept him entertained on long watches and in a small town. "If you're out here then you must be an expert on sand and dust."

Just as I feared, Kamyar's gaze turned to me. "It's more of a historical, religious nature."

Vago laughed and threw an arm around my shoulders. "Then Seja's the worst person to help you. There's no one the Preacher's seen less of."

"Maybe Vago could help you," I said. "There's no one more devout to his drink."

"Then come worship with me," Vago said, tugging me away from the stranger without acknowledging him any further. Vago was always rude like that. Too many people traveled through here to give any special treatment, and their tithes paid for our watch whether or not we were polite to them.

I shot a glance over my shoulder. Kamyar Eirvad stood in the middle of the street, hands in the pockets of his too-clean trousers, a pensive look crinkling the corners of his beautiful eyes.

I followed Vago into the shadows of the saloon. If Mama had something to say to me then she could come herself.

Vago's dusky pithat beer was alone on the counter, half-drunk, until he knocked the bar with the back of his hand and a second one appeared like magic. The bartender Gila winked at me as I slid in next to him, balanced on one of the stools so rickety that only the brave dared inebriate themselves while trying to sit.

"Another pretty traveler for you to tumble?" Vago said, taking a long drink.

I resented how little Vago understood my taste in travelers. I liked my temporary lovers to be pretty, not rich and estranged. "I saw the Preacher today," I said, gazing into the muddy depths of my beer. I wished it were Tila Igala's kokyt tea instead. That always seemed to work better than alcohol at helping me forget my troubles, at least before sleep.

Vago turned to face me fully, any levity gone from his expression. Suddenly I remembered what I appreciated about him — his memory of emotions, mine and his own, that he entrenched in his own heart. He remembered what had happened before. He remembered when Mama left.

"Why did you go?" he said.

I rubbed the handle of my pitcher with my thumb. "Because of those travelers yesterday."

His eyes narrowed. "The ones from San Brado?" I thought he would laugh, or begin another coyote impression, but his gaze was lucid. "I've been thinking about them too. I'm going to go."

"To San Brado?" I had the same urge. "I'll come too."

"No." Vago took a swig from his drink. "Something's amiss with them. Not madness, something more sinister. And it would only help their plans to take away another watcher. You need to stay. Besides, Tifero went on resupply to San Brado a week ago, and it's time he returned. I'll ask him what happened."

Vago sounded so certain that I didn't want to voice the image that rose in my mind of a black hole in the earth where a city used to be. Where our friend used to be.

I brought my pitcher to my lips and gulped it down until cheers from other patrons knocked me out of my escape.

Vago grinned, clinking his drink to mine. "Yes — let's celebrate putting this madness to rest."

I grinned, but I couldn't quite put it all behind me yet. I wanted to see San Brado with my own eyes, but Vago was right. I had to stay. There had to be some other way to shake this feeling.

"Do you believe we have gifts?" I said. "That the Heavens manifest in us?"

"Like Maron?" Vago said, and I instantly regretted asking. Luckily he shook his head and took another sip as if to wash away her name. "No, I don't think it works as simple as that, like they claim. Sometimes it's a feeling, a suspicion." He rubbed his thumb against his fingers, examining the change in dirt on his hands. "I know it doesn't seem it, but I do have faith, Seja. It's just smaller."

*

The Heavens asked Mama to leave me when I was fifteen. This story is different depending on who's telling it.

Tila Igala has an easy fix for everything; kokyt tea. When Mama left and I came to stay with her, she brewed me a cup every night, sifting the dried bitter leaves (sweetened with rose blossoms when we could afford them) into their little satchels and bathing them in steaming water. She didn't make me talk about anything but she would talk at me.

"Your Mama is gone," she said that first night, watching me swallow the scalding tea as if it could burn the hurt out of me. She never stopped me from committing foolishness but would always patch me up after. I'm not saying it was healthy, but it made me not hate her. "But we're not like her."

I nodded. It was enough, for that moment. Tila Igala is my

Mama's sister but in a strange sense, like a moon reflected on rippling water. They only look alike in their full cheeks that I didn't inherit. I don't quite understand the love they had for each other but it was enough for Tila Igala to love me.

After that I found my own rhythm with my sadness. It was everyone else who wanted me to keep tempo with the life we'd had before. Tila Igala still wanted me to come pound dough in the low hot kitchens with the other cooking women. My fellow watchers wanted to keep up target practice, tormenting innocent pebbles. That was when it was just me and Vago sticking together out in the sands, before Tifero came years later, orphaned and inserting himself into our friendship as if he had always been there.

What became comforting to me was anything unusual and erratic. I looked for faces that weren't familiar. I tried aiming my pistol with my other hand, but stopped after Vago's teasing. I stared at the black-ash walls and willed new patterns to reveal themselves to me even though the curves of that wood is more familiar to me than my own skin. At one point I was practically begging the Heavens to send us outlaws, a swarm of them, enough to provide a real challenge. I had daydreams of getting swallowed up by the storm, unable to shoot at them all, gleeful at being taken by surprise.

I was getting itchy. It was the same kind of restlessness that leads to young folks starting fires, so that was why I went to the Preacher for the first time.

It was a Wednesday, when there usually aren't services. I found her sitting on the floor in the middle of the aisle surrounded by a circle of books. When I entered, trying to shut the door as quietly and piously as possible, she scrambled to her feet faster than I thought her age would allow.

"I was wondering when you were coming, Seja," she said, like she was happy but also trying to sound disapproving. "I thought Maron would have sent you right away." She took my hands in hers.

"Mama's gone," I said slowly.

"Yes," the Preacher said, equally slow, as if it was I who wasn't understanding. "She is gone, but you're going to join her soon."

To me, that sounded like a threat, because Mama leaving was a horrible thing. I wasn't going to do the same.

"Dear girl, she really didn't tell you?" The Preacher must have been able to interpret my scrunched up face. "She has been *chosen,* Seja. And soon you will be, too — we will begin our studies so that you can hear the Heavens better, and prepare."

"To leave San Orgafi?" I wished she'd let go of my hands.

"Well, eventually," the Preacher said, hearing the uncertainty in my voice. "It depends on what the Heavens ask of you."

"The Heavens are asking me to give up the watch and come in here to read old books?"

The Preacher sighed. "This is beyond the simplicity of watch. This is glorious, Seja. Of course we didn't expect — well, it really does show that any family can ascend to a greater calling, hmm? Come back tomorrow." She patted my hand. "I will get everything ready for your studies."

I was relieved when she freed my hands and returned to

her books. I walked out backwards, looking up at the slant of sunlight through the rare red glass above her.

I didn't go back to the chapel for nine years.

*

The next survivors were not as composed as the women from San Brado. The day after Vago left, I was on duty alone as a pack of children approached from the northwest.

They followed no road, stumbling over the sand. Some were crying. All were covered in blood and dust. They were led by a skinny young man who had a bandage wrapped around the stump of his missing arm and another around his thigh.

"What happened?" I said, holding out my hand and then placing it back on my belt. My weak heart.

"We're from Penulma," the boy said, coughing. They did look sick, not with disease, but that persistent throat soreness from smoke. "There was..." he trailed off.

My heart slowed as I lifted my gaze to the stretch of sand behind them, searching for a giant shadow, bracing for the ground to shake under monstrous steps.

"Spider," said a little child behind him, grasping at the air with clawed fingers.

"No, Tarantula," said a girl from the other side, looking behind them at the desert. "It was a tarantula because it was hairy."

"A spider as big as the sky," the first child muttered.

"Come inside," I said. "Quickly."

*

Tila Igala can make multitudes out of nothing. She said she befriended a trickster spirit in her girlhood who liked her better fat, so he always kept her well-fed, enchanting grains of rice to multiply when she wasn't looking and her dried meats to regrow overnight. As a child I found this imagery unappetizing, but I didn't question her magic. Now I know it probably has more to do with her network of suppliers that travel through San Orgafi and the connections she has with the other citizens, the ones who live and work here for a lifetime without the luxury of passing through.

In the eyes of these small survivors from Penulma I could see the same childlike enchantment I once felt at the sight of her cooking. A girl with short braids took a bowl of rice from me, eyes wide at the simmering strips of beef among the greens in its center.

"Long way from Penulma," Tila Igala whispered to me, quietly so the children couldn't hear. They were all crowded into her house, a wooden building that doesn't lean as much as the others. The tall boy who led them here was sitting in the corner staring at nothing. He seemed to be the oldest but also the least helpful.

"Several days," I said, watching him. "They said the same thing as those travelers from San Brado."

"What travelers?" Tila Igala spooned out more rice, even though the child nearest her still had a heaping pile. I watched her for a moment. Her hair is straight like mine and she wears it in three long braids that meet at the end behind her back. I wondered how long Mama's hair was now. Then I got mad at myself. It had been a while since I'd had any kind of foolish thought like that. I could only blame that stranger for bringing up her name again, and the unsettling feeling these young folks were giving me.

"We sent them on their way," I said. "They didn't want to stay anyways. They only wanted to warn us."

Tila Igala straightened, wiping her hands on her threadbare apron. Then she took my arm and led me out of the main room, closer to the door, where the sunlight snuck in through the wooden slats in the walls.

"What did they say, Seja?" she said, her dark eyes trapping me like a rabbit in a snare.

I thought it was embarrassing to describe these things to the Preacher, but it was nothing compared to Tila Igala's shrewdness. "They said the same thing as these children. That creatures the size of cities were—"

"My child," Tila Igala said, putting her hands on my shoulders. They weighed me down, kept me tethered to the earth. "My Seja. You are my kin. So was your mother. I watched her fall for these visions. I watched the Preacher drive her to madness. I didn't stop her, but I will protect you." She tilted my chin up. "In times of trouble like these, at the sight of so much suffering, I know how tempting that so-called Holy Word is. But those rich folk in the chapel are not our people. They haven't spent the long hours under the sun like you and I. They aren't here washing and feeding these children now. Of course they have visions, of course they spin tales, when they don't see enough of the strangeness of the real world."

I watched the sunlight paint bars across her face, diving into the hollows beneath her eyes and the curve of her chin.

How many similar shapes did I have? How many did Mama? I hadn't looked in a mirror for so long.

"Alright, Tila," I said. "It's just spooky, is all."

She rubbed her thumbs across my shoulders. "You encounter enough spookiness in your work, I imagine. Now go borrow some cups from Perria so that we can make enough tea tonight for all these little ones. Come back before your watch."

I nodded. As I creaked the door open, I looked back one more time at the skinny boy from Penulma. He was looking at me now, but his gaze was just as empty as before.

*

The next day, after helping Tila Igala stir massive cauldrons of stew for the children, I went down the road far from the main gate. I slid a coin to the innkeeper and stomped up the rickety steps to knock on one of the few doors in San Orgafi that doesn't have splinters.

Kamyar Eirvad answered in a state of undress, his hair mussed. His shirt was gone, suspenders hanging around his hips, a towel slung around his neck. He held a straight razor and half of his sharp jaw was covered in shaving cream.

"Well," he said, tapping the side of the razor against the door. "How did you find me?"

"Tell me what my Mama said to you." I tried to keep my gaze up as high as I could, ignoring the bare expanse of his chest, even though I'm mortal and I can appreciate the Heavens' creations when they're built like that.

"As you can see, I wasn't expecting visitors," he said, still not moving aside to let me in. Even though he was the one half-undressed, he was appraising me, taking in my short sleeves and the absence of my hat. I'd run straight over from Tila Igala's without my usual accoutrements, though my pistol still kept a comforting weight at my hip.

"You were so desperate to find me," I pressed. "And you knew my Mama. Now's the time to tell me whatever strange things she told you."

"I suppose you would know all the comings and goings in this town," he mused, looking down the hall past me. "I just didn't expect you so soon."

"It's easy to find you because you're rich," I snapped. "Only a few places in this town that are palatable for people like you."

He looked at me then. I met his gaze, crossing my arms. I was angry, but I couldn't scare him off. I didn't want to admit it, but he was my only clue to what happened to Mama other than Tila Igala and the Preacher. Tila Igala wanted to keep me away from my Mama, and the Preacher wanted to keep me away from my people.

"Come inside then, Seja," Kamyar Eirvad said, widening the door. "And I'll tell you how I got so rich."

I brushed past him. "And about my Mama."

"Yes," he said, shutting the door behind me. "I was never under the illusion that I could escape that particular tale."

The room was nice, like I suspected. More money meant less dust. Airy white sheets were unexpectedly crumpled on the large bed. Figured him for the tidy type. Pale yellow curtains reached into the room, riding the wind. A tall mirror sat on a table opposite the bed, and that's where Kamyar returned, examining the remainder of his unshaved face.

I sat on the edge of the bed, looking away from him and out the open window over the rooftops of San Orgafi. It felt intimate to be part of someone's personal ritual. I liked when folks appeared the way they wanted without any hint of how they got there. I didn't want anyone else to see me washing my hair or buttoning my shirts. For all they knew I appeared on watch every day, fully formed.

But Kamyar Eirvad seemed to have no qualms about letting me witness him in the process of creating himself. As he examined his handsome reflection in the mirror, I let myself glance over too. There were enough muscles on his back and width to his shoulders to convey that he didn't get rich sitting around all day. His black tattoo continued from his wrist up around his left shoulder, spiraling out into spikes.

"There's a price for the visions from the Heavens," he said. "It matters what you do with them."

"I don't believe Mama really had visions," I said, running my finger over his sheets. They were softer than anything I'd ever touched.

"You haven't had your own?" He met my gaze in the mirror, drawing the razor down his face. "The gift becomes stronger in the next generation."

"If it were real, it wouldn't be a gift," I said.

"There must be something blocking them from you," he said, shaking out the razor in his basin.

"Are you calling me a heretic?" I said, not at all offended.

"I'm saying there's something about this place that's preventing you from receiving the messages." He rubbed his face clean and I took advantage of his hidden gaze to admire the movement of his shoulders again. As he turned around and leaned back against the table I looked out the window again, maybe a little too quickly. "But if there is, I know how to unblock it. There's a sacred stone north of here—"

"And what do you know about this desert? What do you know about what's sacred?" I said. Plenty of travelers came through here acting like they knew everything about the world, and it only took a few days for the heat and the isolation to break them down.

"Your mother told me," Kamyar Eirvad said, patiently.

I clenched my fists in the sheets. "She sent you here so I could have access to my visions?"

"No." He didn't look away, watched my face fall in disappointment. I hated having a witness to this. But he didn't demand anything from me as he continued. "Remember how I said there is a price to the visions? You cannot act on them, or if you do act, it must be on the path of the Heavens."

"So Mama sent you because she had a vision of me, and couldn't come herself?"

"No," he said again, softer. "She didn't mean to act on it at all. If she did, she would lose her gift."

I didn't know what to say to that. Didn't know what the right response was to hear that Mama had chosen to leave me behind again.

Kamyar knelt down in front of me. He didn't touch me but brought his face to the same level of mine. "But I am the one who records the visions in our temple. And I decided to act."

"Why?" I said. It felt hollow to hear him say that. He

wasn't family. "Because I'll have stronger visions than her? Because the Heavens sent you?"

"Because you never should have been left behind," he said, and faith was shining out from his face, though I wasn't sure if it was faith in me or in my mother or in the damned Heavens. "You're meant for something much greater than this place."

"I happen to like this place," I said. *I just wish Mama had stayed.*

"That's why you were chosen. You're a protector. The world is shifting, and you're at the center of it. You have to open yourself up again."

"And then the Heavens will tell me I can't act? I can't save people?" I took his chin in my hand. "You're just a desperate pilgrim, Kamyar Eirvad. The Heavens aren't interested in me. I'm not going to hear anything from them. I can't save anyone more than the folks inside of these black walls."

"And wouldn't it be enough, if you could save them?" He wrapped his hand around my wrist. "If there's a chance you could hear anything, get any warning at all, don't you have to try?"

I pictured a great stretch of fur blocking out the sun, bringing down a city with a howl. Tree-wide spider legs wrapping around buildings and crushing them.

"You came all the way out here to save this little fort?" I said.

"No." His favorite word. His eyes were dilated even in the bright sun, black eating up the brown. "I came to save you."

A pause. I focused on his eyes, on the circle of his hand around my wrist. I wondered if even a madman offering to protect me was better than nobody at all.

Then the warning bells cracked open the silence between us.

I shot to my feet, wrapping my hand around my pistol. Kamyar looked towards the window, unsurprised.

"What is it?" I said. "Another part of the vision?"

"No, it's not time yet," he said. "But you should go." He slid his white shirt off a chair and tugged it over his head. Damn, why didn't he put that on sooner?

I went to the door, and hesitated. "You didn't tell me how you got rich," I said.

He gave me a small smile. "I realize now that I'm not quite ready to reveal such an unflattering aspect of my character."

"It won't be too much trouble to add it to the list of your other unflattering aspects," I said.

He laughed. It was small and controlled and I wanted more. "Would it be too much to hope that I could add to the list of flattering aspects instead?"

I took in his shining eyes, the secretive twist to his lips, the sun threading gold into his dark hair. That list was already worryingly long.

The bells clanged again, and Kamyar Eirvad lay back on his bed, putting his hands behind his head and finally fulfilling the appearance of someone lazy and uncaring.

"You should go protect your town, Seja," he said. "After all, I'm in it now."

*

When I reached the wall the gate was wide open. I raced towards it, almost sending a lady and her skirts tumbling into the dust. Familiar voices shouted down the road. I didn't expect them back so soon. One voice was Vago, engaged in a heated argument with two other watchers, and the other—

"Tifero!" I darted towards his lanky form. He returned the embrace with a startled *oof*. I knew my reaction was over-dramatic, but my friend's return settled the worry and images of giant creatures that had been churning through my mind. I pulled away from him, smiling, and then saw that half of his face was missing.

The right side of him was burned, the black and red scar going down his neck and shoulder. The hollow where his eye had been was now covered with a threadbare patch. The corner of his lips twisted into the scarred skin there, stark against the light tan of the other side of his face.

He grinned, a lopsided thing. "Did you miss me, Seja?"

All the fear came flooding back, the feel of the ground ripping open with giant claws, the wind carrying ancient cries of warning. "What did this to you?"

Tifero frowned. "What?"

"Who," Vago said, striding forward. "The outlaws."

"What?" I said again, unable to look away from the burns on Tifero's face, even though I'm sure it was rude. Twin images of him swam before me, same smile, but the original had *two* hazel eyes, had *two* ears that stuck out slightly.

Vago took my arm. "Our friends from the other day weren't mad."

The travelers. "What do you mean?" *The creatures are real?*

Tifero and Vago exchanged a look.

"Let's get me a drink," Tifero said, putting his hat on again and casting the uninjured part of his face in shadow. "And we'll tell you about the scam of the century."

*

"Imagine the possibilities of an empty city," Vago said when they'd finished. His pithat beer was untouched for once. "No people, no enforcers. Everyone frantic, leaving behind their possessions. Banks and storehouses unprotected."

"I still can't believe they pulled it off," Tifero said. "Convincing nearly everyone that a giant coyote was coming. I should have been more suspicious. The chapels were overcrowded. Preachers out on the streets. But I thought the world was always ending for people like that, so it didn't seem strange."

I stared into my drink as if it would reveal a vision of San Brado still standing.

"And your face?" I said.

"Encountered the outlaws on my way out." Tifero drew his finger down the side of his burnt face. "They said, 'You're too handsome, we can't let you live.'"

"And now?" Vago said.

Tifero took another gulp of pithat beer. "Now, even more handsome. Everyone loves a scar."

"They don't love someone idiotic enough to get one."

My thoughts drifted away from their arguments. I could still see the two travelers clearly, in all black like a warning. They had come to scare us so that we would leave our city unprotected. They meant to return and pillage us, probably with more of their kind.

"So they'll come back," I said to my drink.

"No, we mean to hunt them." Tifero took a long gulp and set his pitcher back down. "No telling how many other forts they've tried to fool. Best to capture them as soon as possible."

"Penulma," I murmured.

"What about Penulma?" Vago leaned in, as if to tug me out of my reverie with his gaze.

"There's refugees here — all children. Except for one boy, older. He led them here."

Tifero finished his drink, slammed it down. "Then that's their accomplice. Let's go arrest him." He strode out of the saloon. His encounter with the outlaw's fire didn't seem to have slowed him down at all.

I grabbed Vago's arm when he started to follow. "They're children. I don't think they're part of this."

He shook his head, fixing me with those patient dark eyes. "That's why they sent them, Seja. They expect you to say exactly that."

I watched them stride out into the sun in possession of all the answers. So there were no great creatures, only false tales spread by bandits capitalizing on the same kind of religious fervor my Mama got drawn into.

But then what was this itch under my skin, that empty gaze in that child's eyes? Why did I keep looking at the walls as if something was waiting behind them? Vago and Tifero would track down the outlaws and there would be answers that way.

But there was one more person with answers. One more way to put it to rest.

I drained my pithat beer and tripped outside into the light. For the second time that day I barreled up barely creaking stairs, threw open the splinterless door without knocking. This time I did expect to catch him unawares since it was almost evening. But Kamyar Eirvad was fully dressed, wearing a dark blue coat, bent over an array of circular silver instruments on the table by the window. When he turned around he did not look surprised to see me.

"Let's go to this fucking sacred stone," I said.

*

At night the sand looks as black as the sky, especially with only the sliver of a moon we had to guide us. Every step past San Orgafi's gate made me feel like I was walking into a wide mouth. Down the throat of some future waiting to swallow me up.

"How can you tell direction in the dark?" I said, looking over at my companion. Kamyar had a long black bag slung across his back. The wind fluttered his night-blue coat open like wings. A flash of silver in his hand matched the glint of his grin.

"We're not the only ones awake," he said, pointing up. I craned my neck to take in the stars. I'd never needed much more from them than decoration, sometimes inspiration for games during late night watches. I'd never thought they might map a path away from the fort. I wondered who else was gazing up, calculating their relationship to the sky with similar silver instruments. Who was heading home or who else was leaving it.

"*Seja!*"

The scream was sudden, loud and shrill. I looked back, slipping in the sand, squinting towards the spiky blot of the fort. I couldn't recognize the voice. It could've come from the Heavens themselves.

Kamyar paused too, watching me. I stared at the sharp outline of the city, waiting to hear my name again, but it didn't come.

"Do you want to go back?" he said, low and patient.

"No," I said. "I'll see this through. Besides, it was probably just temptation trying to lead me out of the Heavens' path." I strode past him. That voice scared me, but I knew if I went back now I would never know for sure. I wouldn't be able to sleep even with enough kokyt tea to fill a river.

After a moment Kamyar caught up, sliding slightly as we hiked up the side of a dune. "I didn't realize you took the Preacher's words to heart."

I was annoyed again at how he'd startled me in the chapel. "Why should I?"

"She's partly right but mostly wrong," he said, catching up to walk beside me. We both had to be careful, stepping on the dark sand. "An inevitable ratio, the more time you spend with books."

I fixed him with a glare. "Don't know if I should be trusting a man who's so distrustful of books."

He tilted his head towards me. "A surprisingly protective instinct from someone who can't read." Even in the dark I could sense his focus. He was a critical, analyzing creature, and I was sure he could make out every speck of dust, every freckle, every thread of me. I didn't ask to be examined, let alone judged, but I couldn't help but hold my breath for the verdict when he continued, "Would you like to learn?"

"Seems like it would only make my world more confusing," I said. I tried to look back at him as carefully as he was looking at me. Unfortunately I couldn't find much amiss with his appearance. I'd have to find fault with him elsewhere. "Since there's so many 'partly right and mostly wrong' books out there."

"I'll help you tell the difference," he said, and there was that grin again, sharp and white as the thin moon.

"Oh, look at that! I've had a vision!" I stumbled in the sand and grabbed his shoulder. His expression immediately turned concerned as he wrapped an arm around my waist and the other around my hand to hold me up. I didn't want to admit that those places where he touched me felt like fire.

I looked up at him, making my eyes as pleading as possible. "I've had a vision that you try to teach me how to read, Kamyar Eirvad. And then...and then I hit you on the head with a book!"

His laugh rippled through both of us. It was louder now, out here in the desert, but still not enough for me. I guess I'm always destined to be hungry for something.

"Yes, Seja," he said. "I'm sure that's exactly how it will happen."

*

I didn't know much about Mama before she left. I was getting older, tasting independence, spending as much time as I could outside the walls. She was inside too much for me to be interested in what she was doing. Holed up with the Preacher and her books. Some nights she wouldn't come home. Every time she tried to cook something it would be burned, and that's why I have a preference for char on my meat.

I remember she had bad dreams.

*

The moonlight carved the stone out of the desert as we approached. It was smoother than the sand around it and twice our height. It looked like concentric rings stacked on top of each other, getting smaller near the top. The shape was familiar to me for some reason, but I shook off that feeling. I didn't want any sort of similarity between me and something sacred.

We stopped a few feet away. I squinted, wondering what color it would be in the light. "Did someone carve this?"

"I don't know." Kamyar approached it, braver than me. There was something strange about that rock. He ran his hand over the ridge closest to him. "There's records of it in the temple. It's too old to have a name and not old enough for the priests to care where it came from."

"What is it supposed to do?"

"Not everything is meant to be used," he mused. "It's about place, about the energy that gathers. The same energy that travels through you from the Heavens."

I wrinkled my nose. "I don't want any 'energy' traveling through me."

"Ah, wonderful," he said, circling around the stone. My heart did a strange drop during the second he was on the other side of it, out of sight. Then returned to normal when he reappeared. "So we've come here for nothing. Turn around, then. Start walking now."

"Stop acting like I'm so easily spooked." I dropped my own pack in the sand and strode towards the rock.

"Then stop acting so spooked," Kamyar said, keeping his hand on the stone as I approached. I paused just an inch away from it. He raised an eyebrow when I didn't make any further movement.

"I don't want to touch it," I said, bracing for another sarcastic remark.

Instead his gaze turned pensive. "Perhaps we should honor that feeling for now." He drew away from the stone, and I felt immediate relief as his skin left its surface.

I tried to look calm as I increased my own distance from it. "What now, then?"

"You'll likely be the next one to give instructions," he knelt beside his pack. "The Heavens speak through you, now."

I watched the curve of his back, his careful fingers undoing the ties of his bag. "Who did they speak to before?"

His hands stilled, fingers curling around another one of his silver globes.

I stepped through the sand, circling him and then crouching down to face him. "Did the Heavens speak to you before, Kamyar Eirvad?" His eyes were unreadable in the night. "Then why did they stop?"

His laugh was the hollowest I'd ever heard it. "I told you I didn't want to add to my list of unflattering characteristics."

I didn't like that distance in his voice. I let my knees hit the sand, brought my body forward. "Would you like me to flatter you, then?"

He breathed in sharply. I didn't feel any of the Heavens now. I felt more like temptation. Maybe I was scared to face them after all. All I knew was that I was glad to get away from that rock, and wanted to keep him away from it too.

And maybe I did know some flattering aspects of him after all.

I raised my hand through the dark, let my thumb rest in the curve beneath his full bottom lip, let my fingers outline his cheek. It was the perfect place to feel the shape of his smile.

"Go on," he said. "I'd love to hear anything complimentary from someone who seems to think so little of me."

I moved closer, bringing up my other hand to cup his face. His arms snaked around my waist. His lips parted, his eyes lowered, down towards my mouth then back up to my gaze again.

"The problem, Kamyar Eirvad — " I tilted his face up, let the moonlight in so I could see the shine in his eyes, " — is that I've been thinking about you a lot."

Another smile curled his lips, and I felt it through my fingertips. "Are you only doing this because you want to know why the Heavens left me?" he murmured.

"The Heavens have nothing to do with this." I brought my lips to his, and he drank me in like a desert during rain.

*

Another memory of Mama. I was thirteen and had my first kiss in the space behind the fort wall and the kitchens. A visiting traveler boy. I never meant to tell her about him, but she caught us. At that age I was convinced that my whole life was destined for embarrassment.

"I saw him," she said when I stormed back inside. The boy got scared off when she opened the door with a slam, interrupting us.

"I don't care if you saw him," I said, wishing I could go to target practice, but my pistol was locked up and only used when I was supervised. "He's passing through. He's not important."

"Not that boy," Mama said, smiling as she shook her head. "The man in your future. He's in a forest, now, surrounded by so much green. He's meant for you. I can't wait for you to meet him."

I faced her. She looked so satisfied, sitting in front of the window with the sun haloing her. Her eyes were darker than mine, her chin thinner. She was looking through me into a time beyond us. If I was only a little younger I would have screamed, *Look at me! Stop spying on my future self!*

I wasn't impressed with Mama or her prophecies. She wasn't wise for knowing what hadn't happened yet when she didn't even know that her child wasn't really a girl, didn't know how good of a shot I was, didn't know that I liked red more than blue or dusk more than dawn.

*

I let Kamyar Eirvad sleep while I couldn't. It wasn't the first time I'd buried my feelings in kisses and skin. After that first unimportant boy when I was young there had been more unimportant boys, an endless stream of travelers to distract myself and prove to Mama that there wasn't anyone important in my future. Sometimes I would sleep with them. Sometimes I'd let them do worse things, like say they loved me and they would stay in San Orgafi forever, until eventually I became numb to that kind of promise.

While we lay there I felt like a shell in the ocean. I've never seen it, but Tila Igala had. She'd describe the tide to me, how the sea brings things from the center of itself to the sand, how it pulls others back. Kamyar Eirvad was like the shore beside me, his arm heavy and anchored around my side. His dreaming breath a constant lull.

But then there was the pull of the sacred stone, a tide tugging at me. The fear of it and the desire at the same time. The moon was behind it now, sideways, bisected, so that the stone had two silver horns.

I lifted Kamyar's arm delicately, rolling out from under his warmth. How tempting it was to stay that close to him out here in the desert, away from the gaze and judgement of San Orgafi. But that wasn't why I was out here.

I tugged on my pants and shirt but left my pistol behind. A strange wind started up, billowing my sleeves and tugging my hair into my eyes. I walked through it and stopped in front of the stone.

Maybe there was some symbolism behind the curves of it, the way it rounded in ridges and ended small at the top. But I wasn't a scholar or even a believer. I was just someone trying to talk to a rock.

Vago had said his faith was small, that it appeared to him

in suspicions. I didn't believe faith could be small — it could only consume you, or be destroyed.

I flexed my fingers, and then, before I could second guess myself, I pressed both my hands flat against the stone.

It felt wrong. That little buzz, the layer of my skin that me and the other watchers had cultivated to keep us on alert, was screaming at me. But I stayed close, dug my fingers in, waiting to see something. Waiting to see a vision of San Brado, or Penulma, or San Orgafi, or me, or Mama.

And then I realized I didn't care about any other forts or towns or even the world. I wanted to see Mama. Was she kneeling in some distant chapel, hidden from this same night sky? Was she in a place with more green? Did she have my name written somewhere, to remind her? Did she ever replay her own memories of me?

"Show me," I said to the stone. *If I'm supposed to be so chosen then why won't you show me?* No, I didn't want to see her. I wanted to know where she was so that I could go to her, so that I could demand answers. Or maybe just to face her. To see what she would do confronted with someone grown up now. Someone who shared the shape of her eyes.

For a moment I thought it was raining and then I realized I was crying. I stumbled away from the stone as if burned.

"Fuck." I turned away, frantically wiping my eyes. When had I last cried? Not over Mama. Not because of dust or long days. Not from Tila Igala's small kindnesses or Vago's loyalty or Tifero's antics.

I wasn't crying now because of Kamyar Eirvad or visions or even Mama. I think I was crying because I was alone. When you're around so many people all the time, new people coming in every day, you can forget that none of them are the one you really want to see. You can pretend that person is still there. You can trick yourself into thinking if you just go looking you'll be able to find them. But here I was out in the desert, being all holy in front of a sacred stone, getting as close as I could.

And Mama was never going to be here with me.

I gulped in air in between my sobs and became aware of a shadow on the side of the stone by me. The long shape of Kamyar Eirvad stretched out, leaning against the rock, his sharp profile pointed towards the sky.

"It started with my grandmother," he said, and I closed my eyes, grateful he couldn't see my tears and grateful that he didn't ask for an explanation. "That's when the temple first started taking notice. Keeping record. Testing her children, and their children." He ran a hand through his hair like I had hours before, mussing it even further. "So of course my father expected his children to have the gift even more than he did. But one after another, they had nothing. All six of them. Disappointments."

I wrapped my arms around myself, gazing up at the moon while he spoke.

"He was getting frustrated, angry at his children who were cut off from the Heavens. It couldn't have been something he did, no, he was a pious man. There was something wrong with all of them. Until me." He stared up at the sky, his thick lashes unblinking. "You would think I would be treasured by him, right? The long awaited child with the gift."

I held my breath. I didn't have the gift, but what if I did? Would Mama have stayed?

"When I was ten I was tested. That's when they took me away to the temple in the mountains. I tried to escape so many times. Carved holes out of the gold-plated walls and stole donkeys to try to make it down the thin mountain paths. Burned Holy Books." I let out a surprised breath, and Kamyar tilted his head towards me, giving me a sad smile. "Yes, even me, the reader. But I wanted to hurt them. I thought the priests had taken me away from my family."

He slid away from the rock and came towards me. He swallowed, put his hands in his pockets. "But I learned that's not what had happened. My father sold me."

I didn't move, didn't say anything. I lifted one hand, hesitant, unsure if it would be enough. He took it and held it up in the moonlight, tracing the lines on my palm with a single fingertip, focusing on that instead of meeting my gaze.

"What's one child, one of many, compared to riches?" He followed the length of my lifeline. "Well, then I decided, what are parents compared to riches?" Here he shot me a roguish smile, and I saw a flash of another side of him, a spirit more similar to an outlaw than a rich man or a priest. "The Heavens showed me another temple, one even deeper into the peaks, overgrown with vines. Perhaps they meant for me to lead the chosen there, to make it sacred once again."

"I suspect that's not what you did," I said, trying to sound light, to hold onto that smile.

"I went alone, but with enough donkeys to carry back what I would find." He held my hand higher until I was holding moonlight. "Seja. What treasures I found — rubies bigger than your hand, emeralds wider than your eyes. Spider-silk robes, tents fit for kings embroidered in their entirety, statues carved so gently they looked alive. I couldn't take all of it at once, of course. But I went back over the years. I accumulated my wealth, made a name for myself in Basang, the city in the foothills of the mountain. I made enough to commission a golden statue." his trickster-grin widened. "It was of me."

I laughed, surprised. He was rich and he was pretty, but he still didn't seem the narcissistic type. "Why?"

"I gave it to my father." I sobered, but his expression wasn't serious. "Since he loved treasure so much. And so that he would never forget me."

I could picture Kamyar's disheveled father and all his children in a rich house, with a great golden statue of his seventh son reminding him of his greed.

"I wonder if I should send Mama a golden statue of myself," I said, trying to join in the joking, but talking about her still gave me a weight in my stomach.

"She believed," he murmured. "I don't know if that's just as bad as greed. But it's why she left."

I drew my hand away from his. "So you had a vision, and instead of following the Heaven's path you stole from the old temple. That's why the Heavens stopped speaking to you? That's why you came to find me, so that I could talk to them for you?"

"I don't care about the Heavens, personally," he said. The wind spiraled his hair out around him, but his gaze was still. "They've only ever led me and my family astray. But whatever you choose to do, Seja — you should at least listen to them first."

"I can't hear them," I whispered. "I don't have the gift." I was only going to think the next words but I let them spill out instead. "I think Mama knew that, and that's why she didn't take me with her."

He snapped into action, folding me into his arms. I stiffened. Even though we'd done far more intimate things earlier this didn't feel familiar. Then his thumb was rubbing circles on my back, and I could feel his breath on my shoulder, his soft hair against my cheek. Maybe I could be protected by something like this, not ash-black walls, but something alive and feeling and soft like me.

"She left because of who she is, not because of who you are. There's nothing you can do in this world to make people like that love you," he murmured. "It will never be enough. That horizon will never get closer."

"I can't stop reaching, though," I said, letting my hand come up and rest on his waist. I leaned my chin on his shoulder and looked up at the dark sky.

"You can. You can stop and choose a place that feels right and make it a home. Make it enough, with or without them." His words reverberated down my back.

"And were you happy in the home you made, Kamyar Eirvad?" I said.

He pulled back, rested his hands on my arms. "You're right, it's never that simple. I suppose I'm still looking for it." A soft smile, and he freed a strand of hair that was caught in my wet eyelashes. "Why do you always say my full name?"

"Because I like the taste," I said, and he laughed. Fully, deeply, wonderfully. There was little I believed in when it came to people or the Heavens or myself, but that sound I would follow anywhere. I would stay anywhere for it.

He curled his hand around my neck. "Then it's yours, Seja Bela Arantija."

"Ugh, not the middle name."

"Convince me otherwise," he said, and kissed me.

*

For a while after Mama's vision about the man in my future I was determined to avoid him. If anything she said came true that would mean she was right, and she was never right. She was spiraling into madness and religious fervor just like Tila Igala said. I really did try to fall in love with those travelers, just to spite her vision.

But I guess it didn't matter if I proved her wrong. She wasn't here to see it. And maybe the best way to spite her would be to be happy after all.

*

We lay out the blanket he brought, agitating less sand this time when we brought ourselves together again. But I still couldn't sleep. This time he didn't either, watching me. I felt at least comforted to know I wasn't alone in the realm of the waking.

"It seems San Orgafi has a choice," I said. "The world's either ending or it's not. A giant creature is going to eat us or outlaws are going to raid us."

Kamyar didn't answer as I spoke to the sky.

"Vago means well," I continued. "He only wants to protect our city. Just like Tila Igala wants to protect her people, the workers, whoever isn't rich enough to leave this desert. And the Preacher wants to protect the chosen. And you, Kamyar Eirvad." I turned to him, watched the stars outline his cheekbones and the curve of his lips in silver. "You want me to protect the chosen of the chosen?"

"You shouldn't say it so accusatory," he murmured. "When you're one of them." His eyes were smaller nights, miniature moons illuminating the corners, his irises dark and drinking me in.

I tilted my head back again to look at the wider sky. "Is there a path that will let me protect everyone?"

"That's what your mother wanted," he said. "She wanted to protect the entire world."

My vision blurred as I focused on the moon and not him, silent as I pictured myself as a small creature, years ago, my hand slipping out of hers, unimportant in the face of everything else, a part of the world but not the part worth protecting.

*

I dreamed. First it was stuck in a loop. I saw a small plant with soft, oval green leaves, catching fire by itself and then burning up into nothing. Again, and again. Growing out of the ground, short and gentle, and then the heat of fire. I tried to save it but then I felt a strange comfort as it burned. As the flames ate away at it I found I could breathe easier.

Then the plant burned into sand instead of ash, and that sand washed into a desert, my desert. The pointed black walls of San Orgafi clawed up through the sand as if they were growing too.

I wasn't walking towards them like a traveler, but floating. The closer I got the higher I rose, even though I reached out, tried to see a familiar face. I flew higher, my body becoming the sky, my senses the stars. I saw the sacred stone. I saw the red-gold dunes marred by the black freckle of San Orgafi. I saw the curve and shift of them. The shape of them.

Then I saw it. I saw it waiting.

I saw its great eyes open.

*

A gunshot cracked my sleep apart. I rolled over and there was blanket, sand, a body, and no pistol. It was the first time in years I'd woken up without my weapon in reach. I blinked my eyes open and the rising sun was low enough to hit me right in the face.

There were shouts and another gunshot. I was trying to untangle myself from everything and then Kamyar Eirvad extricated himself first, racing towards the top of a dune without a shirt, the sun casting his skin bronze. But no time to admire beauty.

I cursed and threw the blanket off, tugging on clothes as I found them and looking for my damned pistol. There was a *schliiiick* and I turned to see Kamyar pull a dagger out of a harness on his calf, twirling it around his thumb. How had I not noticed that?

My frantic hands bumped something hard and I finally drew out my beloved pistol. I stood, slipping on the unsteady sand, knocking specks off of it and checking the bullet chamber.

A similar click from a few feet away as a pistol that wasn't my own was also cocked. I raised my weapon at the same time as her.

The outlaw from San Brado. She was on top of the dune, her blonde-white hair streaming behind her in the sun like a flag, but her eyes were the opposite of surrender, curved by her smile as she pointed her own black pistol at me.

I may have a weak heart but I don't have much hesitation.

My shot hit the shoulder of her gun arm, sending her weapon flying like an injured bird and throwing her body backwards. I raced up the dune to see her tumble down, a trail of her blood matting the sand.

From up there the whole scene became clear. The other outlaws were wearing mostly black or brown, with rifles across their backs or scattered in the sand. The watchers from San Brado were toppling them, working in pairs and tossing pistols across the sand to each other. They must have been low on bullets. The fighting was close, more punching and finger-nails across skin than gunshots. I spotted the burned side of Tifero's face split by his grin as he knocked an outlaw over the head with the butt of his pistol.

Kamyar Eirvad wielded twin silver flashes as he darted be-tween the outlaws, slicing at ankles and wrists to cripple them and render weapons useless. Another dagger? Where had that one come from? Right when you think you've gotten some-one entirely undressed they still manage to conceal things from you.

A shout, another click of a pistol that carried even over

the noise. Beneath me the blonde outlaw had been drawn up to her feet, pistol pressed to her head by a familiar figure with his black hair tied back. Her followers all caught on quickly, exchanging glances and mutters, dropping weapons in the sand and moving towards each other, shepherded by the watchers.

Vago kept his gun to the leader's head as he looked over his shoulder at me. The sun caught the sweat on his forehead, the glint of his pistol.

"What are you doing out here, Seja?" I must have looked pretty useless to him, standing up there on the dune looking shocked, clothes haphazard.

"Who are you doing?" Tifero chuckled, glancing over at Kamyar's bare chest. Kamyar sized him up, giving his daggers another twirl.

"I was trying to protect San Orgafi," I said, scrambling down the dune. I'd never felt more exposed, without my hat or coat. At least my pistol was with me.

"How can you protect the fort without being in it?" Oh, Vago was mad at me. Maybe he had every right to be. I still wasn't sure what the dream meant, but I had a feeling it was a warning for San Orgafi. I was still dizzy from sleep. I had to figure this out.

"You saw something, didn't you?" the outlaw crooned. Her eyes were alight with mirth, though I don't know what she had to laugh about with a bullet that close to her brain. "A vision of your city?"

Tifero stalked closer, keeping his own gun on hand. "You should give up on your ruse now you're caught."

She turned her gaze to him, scanning his tall form. "My

old friend. Your face is still pretty even after my work. You want to complete the look?"

Tifero's smile was slow, thoughtful. "Or maybe you and I could match."

"By the Heavens," Vago muttered, lifting his pistol against her head. "Let's end this."

I grabbed his arm. "Wait." The outlaw raised her eyebrow at me, looking smug and not at all grateful that I was delaying her death. "Let's take them back to San Orgafi."

"Let's take the outlaws into our fort?" Tifero said slowly, so I could hear my own madness repeated back to me. "And then we can buy them a drink, maybe?"

"I'd appreciate it," the outlaw replied at the same time as I said, "I've got questions for them."

"There's nothing new these folk have to tell you," Vago said. It was the same pitying voice Tila Igala had whenever she talked about Mama.

"Give me one day, then," I said. "And then I'll dispense justice myself."

*

The Preacher wouldn't let Mama in when she first discovered her gift all those years ago. We didn't wear clothes fine enough for chapel or pay our tithe to the Heavens. I was only eleven but I remember her frustration. I remember her visions like riddles. She would always drag me to the chapel when she waited for the Preacher after services and tried to prove her visions.

"The moon will rise yellow," Mama told the Preacher. The next day, "The coyote will howl three times at high noon."

"These are peasant superstitions," the Preacher snapped. "Not signs from the Heavens. I don't tutor dirty folks with lucky guesses."

Another day, and Mama was really worked up about this one, she grabbed the Preacher's shoulders and said, "Please, tonight at sunset — six crows and one dove in the center of them will wait above the gate."

Maybe this vision was specific enough to be impressive or maybe the Preacher just wanted to be rid of Mama once and for all, but she agreed to come and see this miraculous event. Mama washed my hair that evening, humming. I hated baths but I savored the touch of her fingers. That was back when my hair was long, and she braided it away from my face for me.

I didn't want to go with her. The Preacher made me uneasy and I was already afraid of Mama, of the glaze over her eyes, of her sudden proclamations and erratic movements. I wanted to spend more time with target practice. Mama was so distracted, so happy to finally prove herself, that she didn't notice me sneaking the pistol out of the storage chest and into my dress pocket before we left.

San Orgafi was quiet that night. It was low season, and even the buildings were holding their breath, creaking less in an absence of wind. Mama pulled me down the road and stopped in front of the gate. She stared up at the top of the black spiked walls as if she could see the Heavens themselves.

"It will all change after this, Seja Bela," she said. Her eyes were glassy and I squirmed in her grip. "We'll be able to leave this desert. They'll send us to chapels by the sea, to temples of gold. I'll be worshipped."

I looked up at her long hair, wild in the wind. I realized, even then, that she wasn't so devoted to something outside of herself but to her own self.

Then the birds came.

They cawed and I was scared but I still watched. The crows landed out of order, choosing spikes to set themselves on. Mama let go of my hand, held her breath as they lined up, a row of black.

And then, like a falling star, the white dove.

I shivered in the warm night. This last bird was delicate, its wings caressing the night as it fluttered down. It landed on the gate and completed Mama's vision with three black-feathered guards on either side.

Mama let out a giggle-shriek, covering her mouth quickly so she wouldn't scare them off. I stared up at her, waiting for her to look down at me, to celebrate again, to talk about us, about what would change. But she never looked down.

The birds were calm, soft and waiting.

Then the gunshot.

It hit the dove and it toppled down on our side of the gate, wings spread wide. Mama screamed. The other birds took off, rejoining the dark of the night.

Mama clutched at her head and turned around. Her eyes were wide and terrifying. Then they landed on me, finally. On the pistol in my hand.

Mama dug her fingers into my skull and they weren't gentle now. "*What have you done?*" she hissed, and I dropped the pistol and started crying at the pain of her nails. Then we both froze when heavy footsteps came down the road.

The Preacher looked different without her black robes, wearing only a white dress and gray coat. She made her way towards us, not looking at the gate but at Mama with her hands tearing my hair from my scalp.

Mama let me go and I fell into the dirt. I heard her choke on her words, sob, and then she ran down the road past the Preacher. I watched the bottom step of the house in front of me, keeping my cheek to the ground.

Footsteps approached. I saw the bottom of the Preacher's coat brush past towards the gate. I exhaled, watching my breath stir the dust in front of me. Then, a gasp behind me.

The Preacher's footsteps again, this time running after Mama. Once that sound was gone I dragged myself up, rubbing dust out of my now-knotted hair. Mama's careful braids were undone.

I didn't want to go after Mama or the Preacher so I walked towards the gate. As I got closer the dove's body seemed to glow, the only bright thing in the night. I stopped above it, and then I understood what the Preacher had seen.

Six black feathers had fallen along with the dove, lined up on either side. Its wings were spread smoothly out as if it were in flight. My bullet had hit it in its exact center. Its insides were split open in perfect symmetry, bones splintering apart in matching cracked patterns on both sides. Its black dead eyes gazed up at me.

*

Despite my strong words I found myself anxious about questioning the outlaw once we returned to San Orgafi and funneled them all into our small jail. Vago locked the bars, then the door, joining me outside.

"Where's the other one?" I said, before he could start his rant about me leaving last night.

"Which one? All of her kind that we didn't kill are in there too." He twirled the keys around his finger absently, focusing on me as if he could uncover why his closest friend had suddenly gone mad.

"The shorter one who was with her the first day they came." *We have greater things to fear now.*

Vago shrugged. "I'm sure they're running other scams across the east. But outlaws are like mice — just because more will come later doesn't mean you shouldn't kill the ones right in front of you."

"I'm not saying don't kill her," I said, even though I wanted to say that. "I'm saying I have...things to figure out." My whole face was burning from sun and sweat and sand.

"What do you have to figure out?" Tifero came around the side of the building and looked only marginally less exasperated than Vago. There was no sign of Kamyar — when we'd returned to San Orgafi he'd taken off, and I was too preoccupied wrangling outlaws to chase after him. I think that was a good thing. My friends needed me to convince them, not a stranger. "Do you not believe us, Seja?"

I rubbed my face, but that only added more sand to the itch in my eyes. "I just...I had a strange dream, is all."

"A dream telling you to endanger the fort and spare the outlaws?" Vago's voice was unforgiving. "At least your

Mama's visions were never a threat to us."

I looked up at him, stunned. My eyes watered and my friend's sharp face swam in my vision.

"This is real, Seja." Vago grabbed my hand and shoved it against the outer wall. I dug my fingers into the soft black ash. "Those visions make you forget what's right in front of you. They put people in danger. Whatever you saw didn't happen and won't happen. *This* is San Orgafi." He pressed his hand over mine, binding us to the wall as we held each other's gaze.

Tifero put his hand on my arm. "I understand that you want to feel closer to her, but there's no point putting store in dreams over what we've seen with our own eyes."

"And what did you see?" I said to Vago's black gaze. His face swam into focus, his eyes narrowed like knives. "The travelers said there was a chasm where San Brado once was, so what did you see?"

"I found our friend on the road with half his face missing!" Vago drew his hand away from mine and gestured towards Tifero's burns.

"You met on the road and headed back?" I said, letting my hand fall away from the wall. Vago kept his arm pointed at Tifero, straight like a falcon extending a wing. "You never saw San Brado. That's why you returned so quickly."

"I was chasing the outlaws out of town when Vago found me," Tifero said quickly, sensing my anxiety was about to turn on him. "And the city was still standing when I left. It's still standing now, Seja — "

I pushed past both of them, grabbing the keys from Vago. He let them slip out of his grasp like a parent tired of denying a child.

They hadn't seen the city for themselves.

The outlaws' leader was lying against the wall, staring up at the sun through the window high above her. A bandage was wrapped around her shoulder where I shot her, the blood blooming like a red flower. The sun sliced her face in half but she kept her eyes open into it even though that must have burned horribly. Maybe she was preparing for the torture she thought was ahead of her.

I wrapped my hands around the bars. She didn't look up even after I cleared my throat.

"I suppose we could start with your name."

After a moment she replied. "Irayn." A little smile. "You won't mind if I keep my second name to myself, do you? Even this close to death I figure I got to protect myself."

"Name's got nothing to do with protection," I said. "But you might find they're some help in allowing folks to get to know you better."

"Alright then, my nameless jailer," she said, blinking into the sun. "One name's the best you'll ever get to know me."

"I'm Seja Arantija."

"And a lot of good it does me, knowing that." Her words were gentle, her smile curving further.

I couldn't help but have some kind of admiration for her. She was a thief but she was free, making some sort of way for herself without parents or protocol or Heavens. Certainly not the Heavens — if they had a path, I'd never seen someone farther from it.

"Why use the Holy Word to spread your lies?" I said. She kept her eyes focused on the sun. Damn, she'd go blind looking into so much light like that.

"Because folks believe in it," she said. "As they should. It's all true."

My thumb started tapping against the bar. "What's true?"

"The creatures." Now she slid her gaze towards me, blinking in the shadows. She probably couldn't even make out my face. "It's not just happening here, you know. It started in the south, in the jungle. They predicted it a while ago. It's all true." She closed her eyes. "We just took advantage of it."

"You're brave, using your last few words to spread more lies. That or you're committed to your heist. Are others coming? If we leave this city now because of some pretend creature, even if we kill you, will more of you come to raid it?" *Like mice.*

"You tried to convince them, didn't you?" Her eyes remained shut. "And they didn't believe you." She sighed, uncurled her limbs, stretched out as if she were only roused from a comfortable nap and not conversing with someone deciding whether or not to kill her.

"It's good of them to distrust me since I was so close to falling for your story," I said, trying to use the words to lend me more certainty than I actually had. The higher the sun rose, the more distant my dream seemed. The more I was hurt by Vago's disappointment and Tifero's pity. What did it matter if they hadn't seen San Brado? Wasn't a place standing until proven destroyed?

"How desperate we are to prove ourselves to people who don't deserve us." Irayn looked at me now, and there was an understanding there that made me uncomfortable. "We either kill ourselves in pursuing extremes, or figure out they were never worth our love in the first place."

"Sounds lonely to not love anyone," I said.

"I'm not saying that," she said. "I'm saying, why love someone who doesn't love you back?"

I curled my hands around the bars. *Because what else can I do?*

"You could join us, you know." She leaned her head back against the wall again. "Think of the money, stealing from the people who look down on you. You would have enough to travel—isn't there somewhere you want to go, someone you want to see?"

"I want to see San Orgafi safe," I said. But what if I knew where Mama was, what if I had riches, if I had a ship that could brave even the most distant waves...

"Ah, well no one is going to see that happen." And then she chuckled, which turned into a hacking cough. Her wound darkened, the blood spreading.

"Where's your companion?" I said. "The other woman who tried to 'warn' us."

"She's the one with the gift, like you," Irayn said. Then she grinned, though pain was laced through it. "So she's the most afraid. She's a long way from here."

"You really think a giant creature is going to consume this fort?" Before I could stop myself I added, "What kind of creature?"

Irayn's laugh echoed through her cell. "What an interesting question." The sun illuminated the cruel sapphire shade of her eyes. "You already know — you've seen it."

I waited, but her eyes closed again, some strange satisfied

peace falling over her. She didn't tell me what the creature was.

So she hadn't seen it. She couldn't know what my vision had been.

It had just been a dream.

*

I expected Tila Igala's house to be hot and stifling, still filled with the orphans from Penulma, but it was empty when I stepped inside. Vago and Tifero weren't still around when I'd left the jail and there was no sign of Kamyar Eirvad so I'd retreated to the only place where I didn't have to explain myself.

For a moment it was just me and the echo of my bag dropping to the floor. Then my aunt appeared from the attached kitchen, carrying a bag of grains, which she promptly dropped and gasped.

"Seja, my Seja," she said, and I was so surprised at the severity of her reaction that I almost didn't respond when she hugged me. Then my arms came up around her too, patting her soft comforting form and familiar three braids. She pulled back, eyes shining. "I was so worried. I called for you. Didn't you hear? Why didn't you come back?"

I had almost forgotten about the shout of my name that Kamyar and I had heard when we first left the night before. I was surprised she was the one who had made such a desperate sound. "I'm alright, Tila."

"Have strange things befallen you, child?" She rubbed her hands up and down my arms.

"I...no more than usual," I said, still taken aback by her focus.

"Here, tea. I'll make you tea." She swiped at her eyes and hurried away.

"Where are the children from Penulma?"

"They moved on," she called from the kitchen. "Travelers came through and helped them get east. They were all anxious to leave, even though I fed them as much as I could, of course. I don't blame them for getting out of here so quickly after those foolish boys on the watch with you came and tried to 'arrest' them. Your friends have nothing better to do than bother children?" Her words were light and joking but there was a hollowness in them.

I slowly followed her voice, watching her grind up the kokyt leaf and pour it with shaking hands into the tea satchel.

"Are you alright, Tila?" I said.

She let out a laugh-sigh as she set the satchel into a cup. "You had me worried. I thought this would happen sooner after your Mama left, that you'd get the idea to follow after her, to chase spirits of your own. You were so good for so long that I thought you were free from all that."

"I am good, still. I won't do that," I said, and I took the hot tea from her, determined for my words to be true. I raised the cup to my lips, the familiar bitter smell wafting towards me.

A buzz, a warning.

I lowered the cup. Tila Igala watched me, hands clutching her skirt, eyebrows furrowed.

"Tila," I said, looking over her shoulder at the mortar and pestle and dried leaves. "What does the kokyt plant look like?"

Soft, oval green leaves, catching fire by itself and then burning up into nothing.

"What a strange question, child. I get them from the spice trader like everything else. Do you know what all the plants you eat look like? We're in a desert."

"You made this for me every night since Mama left," I said, lowering the cup further, letting it dangle from my fingertips. "Except for last night, when I left."

Tila Igala stared at me, frozen.

I let the cup fall to the floor.

"Seja, please!" she called after me as I ran. I recognized it now, the same voice that had called after me last night. A voice desperate because I'd left. Because I hadn't had my tea.

Because then I would have the dreams.

*

When I burst through the chapel doors I did not expect to see Kamyar Eirvad hunched over a Holy Book at the altar. But it didn't alter my anger.

"Take it," I said, figuring he would be as good as the Preacher for what I wanted.

He turned to me, the red stained glass illuminating his dark hair. Maybe the Heavens weren't talking to him anymore but I had no doubt they had chosen him. I strode towards him, holding my hands out.

"So you did have a vision," he said, closing the book slowly. Why did he still come to the chapel, still read the Holy Word when the Heavens had given up on him?

"Take the gift," I said, my voice cracking. "I don't want it. You can have it."

He set the book down, coming down the steps of the altar towards me. "It's yours, Seja. Just like it was your mother's."

"And look what it did to her." I curled my hands back in towards myself. "I don't want to leave San Orgafi. If I take the gift that means I have to leave."

"Then don't." He came closer. "Do whatever you want."

I laughed, and it was as empty as the chapel around us. "But that's not allowed, is it? I can't stray from the Heavens' path or I'll lose the gift."

"I think I turned out alright after straying," he said with a crooked smile, and then took my hand in his. The black ash from the walls spread between our palms. "But that's why I came for you, Seja. When I saw the record of your mother's vision, that you would be just like her, I wanted you to have a choice. I didn't, at first." I looked up at his solid brown eyes, the certainty in them. "It's not easy to give it up. There is a purpose, an energy. Things that I can't explain, in this path." His eyes strayed back to the Holy Book he had been holding. "But it isn't always the right answer. You can keep your gift and return to the temple with me, or act on it and lose all future visions, but whatever you do —" His grin widened. "Do so dramatically."

It was the sadness in his words, not his smile, that made me certain he understood what he had given up. "Should I construct a golden statue of myself, too?"

"As many as you'd like." His thumb brushed the back of my hand. "I'll finance it. As many jewels and estates and exotic pets as you desire, I'll give you those as well."

What did the world look like beyond San Orgafi? Did I want it? "Why?"

I felt the press of his fingers. That tight grip of not wanting to lose someone.

"Because you're like me," he said. He pressed his lips to my forehead. "I won't leave you, Seja. I'll follow you. My crossroads is behind me. Now I'll follow yours. If your path remains in this dusty city or if it takes you to the ends of the earth."

I stared at the gold thread running through his coat, at the black ash coating our hands.

"Would you take me to see my Mama?"

He pulled away slowly, his gaze searching. "Are you sure that's what you want?"

I wondered what he'd said to his father when they'd reunited. If he'd asked why he'd sold his son to the temple. What could his father say? Was there anything to say that would make it better?

"Where is the Preacher?" I said instead.

Kamyar nodded towards the side door that led to her prayer room. I started towards it, and slowed when I felt his hand drift reluctantly from mine.

I turned back to him. There was a wanting, a question in his eyes. He was always so sure and confident, I'd forgotten he'd had the same choice as me before. Both of us cursed with visions. Because of that power, the world wanted us to choose to save the world, the Heavens wanted us to choose to follow them. But maybe we could choose each other.

I pressed a kiss to his knuckles, where the black spike of his tattoo ended. A promise to the Heavens written on his body, a path that he'd given up.

His fingers tightened around mine before releasing me.

"Find me after," he said, half a question. He watched me walk towards the prayer room. The sun painted the curve of his eyebrow and jaw a deep red from behind the stained glass.

The Preacher's room was dark. Her body could have been a stone, unmoving and curled in on itself in the center of the room.

I stopped beside her. "You must have some advice for me."

"There was no way for me to truly help you until you came to me yourself, Seja," the Preacher said. Her chin was pressed to her chest, hands clasped, old knees bent underneath her on the hard stone. She seemed smaller, somehow, swallowed by her black robe. "You know now that I was never lying, that you were meant for this. Now we can begin. Now I can guide you back to the path."

"Like you guided Mama." I stared down at her round form, daring her to look up at me.

"I told Maron to stay," the Preacher said. "I don't have the gift, but even I could feel that San Orgafi would be in danger some years from now."

"You told her to stay," I said flatly. "And she still decided to leave."

"She had visions of things greater than this desert, a purpose that called her beyond this place. How could I stop her?" The Preacher unfolded and refolded her hands together.

"And what were those things?" I said, my eyes stinging, wondering what could have been wonderful, important, beautiful enough to call her away from me. Would I see something like that in my next vision? Something great enough to call me away from San Orgafi and everyone I loved here?

Now the Preacher looked up. Her smile was a thin crack in her wrinkled face. "You will see them, too. Don't worry. I will help you understand them. I will help you from now on."

"And what if I don't? What if I never have another vision again?" I knelt in front of her. "Will you still help me then? No, I don't think so." I pressed my hand against the smooth chapel floor, where Mama must have prayed for so many hours. "You never wanted it to be me, poor and irreverent. You don't want to help me or help the people of San Orgafi — you only care about the Heavens."

"They are greater than all of us, child," the Preacher said gently. "There is nothing more important."

If I studied with the Preacher I could become important. I could let San Orgafi succumb to this terrible vision and commit myself to the Heavens. I could see the greater world. I could go with Kamyar and gain entrance to the temple and be chosen like Mama. I could see the future alongside her and finally *be* seen.

I flexed my fingers over the stone floor. I could feel it all, as clear as my dream. This smooth stone. The imported pale wood of the chapel. The rich stained glass. The dust of the streets, the creaking doors, the ash-black walls, the sand of the desert. The swish of satin skirts and strange colored dyes on the coats of travelers. Wide hats and new pistols. Pithat beer in the shadows and target practice in the sun.

"I've always been small-minded, Preacher," I said. Ash from my fingertips marred the floor. "I've only ever cared about this city. So if the Heavens take it from me —" I stood, brushing sand off of my coat. "Then I'll burn all of them back down to earth."

I left the chapel. Those pews now empty of tittering rich folk and Kamyar and promises of peace in the next life.

I went down the main road but didn't open the gate, instead sliding into the shadow between the watchtower and the wall. This was always the best place to be for any citizen of San Orgafi. Out of the sun and out of sight.

I dug my nails into the black wood, watched the ash flake down. I drew my gaze up to the spiked top where I had shot down the dove. As I exhaled the wind brushed my short hair away from my face.

Beyond these walls there was the desert, and in that desert something was waiting. I knew it as certain as I knew my own name, as certain as Mama had been when she'd seen those birds in the future. It wasn't the knowing that made us different. It was what we did with it.

I pushed away from the wall and strode back towards the road. I had much to do before the dawn.

*

I love San Orgafi. I love the people in it, even the people just passing through, even the rich folk, even the outlaws, even the ones who loved me and lied to me or the ones who don't love me yet. I love our tall black walls and splinters and creaking steps and dark beer.

But if I have to choose — I love the people more.

*

Kamyar Eirvad is a light sleeper. When I settled myself on the edge of his bed he didn't open his eyes as he murmured, "Seja Bela Arantija."

"Kamyar Eirvad." I brushed a strand of his dark hair, longer than mine, out of his face.

"Well then," he drawled, eyes still closed. "Were you also hoping we might recreate the other night with less sand this time?"

"It's almost sunrise," I said.

His hand snaked around my hip. "Do you only want me under moonlight?"

"Under all light," I promised, and his eyes flickered open at that. An errant sunbeam forged his eyes into copper-gold.

"And what about the dark?" He sat up now, matching my height, using his thumbs to brush the soft space underneath my eyes.

"The dark is our favorite," I reminded him, and then pressed a soft kiss on his lips.

He looked at me strangely as I pulled away. "Are you alright?"

"Yes," I said, weaving my fingers through his. "We just need to go now."

He dressed quickly and unquestioningly, collapsing his silver instruments and swinging his bag over his shoulder.

We walked down the main road. The sun was just waking up, dripping gold into our path, and I sped up as we got to the gate.

"It's quiet," Kamyar said, looking up at a leaning building above us.

"It's early," I said. "People don't have much reason to be awake yet, do they?"

Kamyar frowned at that, but I was a practiced actor by now. And this was my last lie.

We walked south, avoiding the road and heading towards the top of the highest dune above San Orgafi. I wanted the best view.

"What now, Seja?" Kamyar said, softly, not pressing, not mentioning the vision. I'd never told him about my dream.

I raised my hand to block out the sun, let my smile free. We were safe. "Watch."

We had a moment alone with the new sun, and then it matched the same shade of day as my dream.

It started with the sound. The rattle, distant. The earth shook. I knew which direction to look in. The sacred stone was moving closer, thundering, warning. It had always been alive, the rattle at the end of this great creature. The sands between it and us shifted, parted. Then that shaking hit us, and we both fell, slipping on the sand but crawling back so we wouldn't fall down the dune. I got back to my feet first, not wanting to miss a second of it.

It looked like a flood. Blue scales swam up out of the sands. Bluer than the dusty sky had ever been here. Then the eyes, just like in my dream. Gold and bigger than a person.

The snake slid towards San Orgafi.

I tore my eyes away just enough to see my companion's reaction. Kamyar scrambled to his feet beside me, hand on his heart, black hair awry in the wind that was curling around this new shift in the world. His lips were parted, his eyes wide.

"I thought its skin would match the sands," he whispered. "So it could blend in."

I considered the creature as it unspooled its azure scales into the desert. "Maybe the world before had blue deserts and red seas. Maybe the people were giants then, too."

He laughed, full and throaty. It seemed the Heavens were capable of making beautiful creatures in addition to terrifying ones.

You can stop and choose a place that feels right and make it a home, he'd said to me. *Make it enough, with or without them.* I was starting to see the shape of it, that new home, not this desert or distant lands but maybe this person.

"But what about San Orgafi?" Kamyar said, and when he turned to me I saw that he wasn't even worried about the fort, he was worried about me, about how much I wanted to protect it.

I raised my hand, pointed at the dunes east of us. Where black specks of distant crowds were crawling across the sand.

"There's San Orgafi," I said. "You're the last one out."

The first was Irayn the outlaw. I'd freed her and her accomplices in the shadow of night.

Head east, I said. *You're about to be followed, so be as fast as you can.*

Hey, better than being eaten. She winked and stole out of the gate I'd cracked open for them.

Then my friends. I went to Vago first, told him the outlaws had escaped. Promised I'd stay behind with Tifero. He grabbed his coat, his weapons, rushed out to chase them down, but not before he'd turned back.

You're nothing like her, Seja. I know you won't leave us.

I won't. I clasped his hand, squeezed it for luck.

Then Tifero. *The outlaws escaped. You need to track them down, take the other watchers with you. Vago and I will stay.*

Any chance for revenge on that white-haired pyromaniac, Tifero said, always cheerful even after being woken in the middle of the night. I ran my hand across his burnt cheek, and he let me feel the change in his skin. He placed a kiss to my forehead and then grabbed his rifle, stealing out into the night to rouse the rest of the watchers.

Then the Preacher. I did not wake her gently.

It's coming, I said tearfully, shaking her frail form. *Quickly, gather the chosen outside of the city.*

I'm glad you came to your senses, Seja, she said, still finding the time to put on her ceremonial robes. *In times like this.*

Of course, her chosen were the rich folk, the chapel-goers and tithe-payers. They weren't sneaky on their way out of town but that's what I wanted.

Then Tila Igala.

She cried when she saw me, digging her hands into my shoulders and pressing her head to my chest. *I'm so sorry, my child, I'm so sorry.*

You were right Tila, I said, stroking her soft hair. *All of this madness from the Preacher about great creatures — it's a trick. The outlaws are going to raid San Orgafi, and the holy folk have already escaped. They mean to leave the rest of you behind to the violence.*

Tila Igala had the town wrapped around her finger, and the rich folks were already loud with their cases of jewels and brush of silk as they slinked out of town, so it wasn't hard to see that they were up to something. Tila Igala spread the word and helped the rest out, the working folk and the travelers, heading east towards another dune.

And so I emptied San Orgafi.

The snake coiled itself up, forked tongue larger than a building flicking out as it examined the fort. It rattled its tail, the sacred stone now freed from the sand. Horn-like scales on its head pulled back to reveal golden eyes. It was a sidewinder, one of the serpents that knew how to travel across the hot sand quickly and then bury themselves in it to wait for their prey. And this one had waited for generations.

It happened just like my dream, but the difference was I could feel it now. The shaking ground. The shifting sands as the beast slunk closer and widened its mouth.

The sidewinder devoured San Orgafi.

Acknowledgements

Thank you André Alexis, Edie Meidav, Jeff Parker, and Margot Douaihy for your mentorship, guidance, and support for this novella. Christina Sun, Yvette Ndlovu, and Stephanie Santos for reading this during Summer Exhaustion, for your encouragement, and for the group chat. Mark Bias, Mike Zendejas, Alex Terrell -- you know what you did (supported me and my writing and roasted me when necessary). Charlotte Lewis and Lyanne Rodriguez, my day ones. Frankie Diane Mallis, my twin who taught me so much. Nadia Saleh, Natalie Patalano, Christine Bondira, Jessie Farese, Elissa Mallis, Nicole Cantor -- thank you for everything. I appreciate you so much for your cats, couches, and texts. Betsy, Meghan, and Lettie -- love you and your magic family. Matthew and Caleb, love you forever because I'm stuck with you forever. Mom, thank you for being my biggest hype person and for allowing me to check out ten thousand books from the library. Dad, thank you for taking me out in the woods when I was little so I could come up with weird nature stories. Katya, thank you for your excitement and appreciation for literature. Yia yia, thank you for keeping my ego in check. Aunt Krissy, you are my same soul forever, so you already know how much I love you. Thank you Gateway Literary Press and Joe Baumann for selecting this strange little novella and bringing it into the world. UMass Amherst, for the color of your fall leaves and for funding my spooky stories. Brookline Booksmith and Booklink Booksellers for enabling my fiction addictions. Mrs.

Stephens and Readmore Bear for starting that addiction. Mrs. Townsend, thank you for being my book dealer. Ms. Gold and Ms. Pierce for encouraging me to keep writing. Grubstreet, Clarion West, and Tin House, it's an honor to be a part of your community. Thank you to the writers who show up to my classes every week and share their processes, fears, and imagination with me. It's always an honor to learn from and be inspired by you. Lastly, The Roost Northampton, for your breakfast sandwich with rooster sauce (please, tell me the secret recipe) and the wobbly wooden table where nearly all of this novella was written.

Marcella Haddad loves armadillos, Nutella, and the sea. Her prose and poetry have appeared in *Variant Literature, Okay Donkey, Apparition Lit*, and others, and have been nominated for the Pushcart Prize and Best of the Net. She was a Tin House YA 2022 Scholar, and is the Managing Editor of Moonflake Press. She holds an MFA from UMass Amherst and is the author of the micro-chapbook WITCH HOUSE (Ghost City Press) . You can find her in a tree or at marcellaphaddad.com.

Printed in the USA
CPSIA information can be obtained
at www.ICGtesting.com
LVHW021100070524
779602LV00008B/295